Mountain Bike Madness

by Betsy Sachs

illustrated by Penny Dann

A STEPPING STONE BOOK

Random House New York

Library of Congress Cataloging-in-Publication Data
Sachs, Betsy.
Mountain bike madness / by Betsy Sachs ; illustrated by Penny Dann.
p. cm.
"A Stepping Stone book."
SUMMARY: Fourth-grader Billy Getten tries to juggle three jobs—and watch his
younger sister—in order to earn enough money to buy a new bicycle.
ISBN 0-679-83395-1 (pbk.)—ISBN 0-679-93395-6 (lib. bdg.)
[1. Bicycles and bicycling—Fiction.   2. Moneymaking projects—Fiction.]
I. Dann, Penny, ill.   II. Title.
PZ7.S1186Mo   1994
[Fic]—dc20   93-29929

Manufactured in the United States of America   10 9 8 7 6 5 4 3 2 1

To Alison and Walter,
special thanks

1

The warm June sun beat down on Billy
Getten. He leaned over the rusty handlebars of
his secondhand bike and started pumping like
mad to get up the hill. At the steepest part, his
chain guard started clanking. He hated his old
clunker bike.

If only he had one of those all-terrain
mountain bikes! It would eat up this hill.

Billy saw the pothole in the road too late.
Bam! The bike careened out of control and
headed straight for a parked car.

Without thinking he squeezed the hand
brake, but the cable had snapped months ago.
He put his weight on the foot brakes and skid-
ded to a stop inches from the car.

Whoa, that was close! Billy wiped his face

with his arm. Mrs. Lowell would have been steamed if he had bashed her car. He really needed a new bike.

Billy started pedaling. The front rim whined, scraping against the fork. Then the tire went flat. "Swell," he muttered.

There was no way he could ride the bike now. It was the first week of vacation, too! What was he supposed to do all summer?

Billy pushed his useless bike the rest of the way up Lee Avenue. By the time he got home, he was all sweaty. He dropped the bike on the front lawn. The kickstand had fallen off long ago.

"Yo, Bill!"

Billy turned. His best friend, Howard Rosa, came cruising toward him on an all-terrain Lightning Predator. It was a midweight bike, with a wide black saddle, fat chunky tires, and eighteen gears. "Whoa, Howard! When'd you get that?" asked Billy.

Howard did figure eights in the driveway. The Predator's black-and-green finish sparkled in the sunlight. "You like it, Bill?"

"Oh, man! It's beautiful. Is it from Ronson's Bike Shop?"

"I don't know. I got it for my birthday." Howard braked. He rested a sneaker on the curb.

Billy ran a finger over the straight handlebars. There was no rust, and not a dent anywhere on the bike. He tried one of the brake handles.

Howard tightened his green-and-black gloves. "Cool, isn't it?"

"Could I try it?"

"You know how to shift gears, right?"

"Oh, yeah."

Howard watched Billy climb on. "Don't be gone too long."

"Okay," said Billy. He kicked off and slid away from the curb. He was so used to his bike, he wasn't sure he could ride Howard's, but he had to try. And once the wheels started humming, the Predator was bike heaven all the way. This is so easy, he thought.

Billy flew past houses and whizzed around the place where Dr. Mike, the veterinarian,

used to live. At the corner, he turned in to the deserted schoolyard. He almost wished it wasn't summer, so the kids in his fourth-grade class could see him charging around.

Billy circled and headed back to Lee Avenue. Next came the real test: the hill! On his own bike, he'd be panting halfway up.

Billy shifted to a lower gear. The Predator soared. Like no hill at all, he thought. Coming back toward his house, Billy saw Stewie, his black-and-white dog, sitting under a tree with Howard.

Stewie wagged his tail as Billy came to a stop. The dog sniffed at the spokes.

Howard got to his feet. "Is that the best or what?" He reached for his bike.

"I have to have one. Mine's beat."

"Absolutely," Howard agreed. "Well, I better go collect for my paper route. There's this micro-pump helmet I saw at Ronson's. It's got a pump inside it for adjusting the fit. I'm saving up to buy one." Howard climbed on. "Bill, if you get a new bike, we could race through the woods at the reservoir."

"Oh, yeah." Billy sighed.

Howard leaned way forward. "See ya!"

Billy watched him pedal away. Howard was just about the luckiest kid in the whole world. He had a new bike. He had a paper route. His parents let him spend his money on whatever he wanted.

Billy pushed his wheezing bike up the driveway. Stewie trotted along beside him.

"Billy!" his mother shouted. "Come in and watch your sister. Grandpa has to leave now."

"Mom?" Billy couldn't see his mother anywhere.

"Up here." Mrs. Getten stood on the roof, wearing old jeans and rubber gloves.

Dressed like that, Billy thought, she didn't look anything like a kindergarten teacher. "What are you doing?"

"Cleaning the gutters. They're clogged with leaves."

Billy's father was next to the chimney. "Dad!" Billy shouted. "Can I ask you something?"

"Not now!" Mr. Getten yelled back.

"But it's important."

"Later, Billy!"

Not long after, Billy found his father washing up in the bathroom. "Dad, can I talk to you?"

"What's up?" Mr. Getten pulled a towel off the rack.

"Howard just got this new bike, and I was wondering if—"

"Wait." Mr. Getten dried his hands. "Is this about money?"

"Sort of."

"Not a good day."

Billy glanced at his father in the mirror. He wasn't sure what he meant. "Well, see, there's this mountain bike—"

"Billy, we just had a man tell us it's going to cost hundreds of dollars to repair the roof. We can't afford a bike right now."

"But my knees hit the handlebars."

Mr. Getten sighed. "I thought you were saving your allowance."

"I am, but I'll be two hundred years old by the time I have enough. And I'll never be able to go to the movies again."

"Billy, sometimes you have to make choices."

"Boy! Howard's so lucky. He gets everything he wants. All he has to do is *want* it."

"It doesn't work that way, Billy. People create their own luck."

Billy rolled his eyes. His father always said junk like that. Down the hall, Billy's baby sister started crying.

"You know, your mother and I would like it if you'd watch Sarah when we have work around the house. We can't keep asking Grandpa to come over here all the time."

"Would you pay me?"

"No, that's just part of being in a family. But you could earn money by doing extra chores."

"Like what?"

"Your grandmother needs help with the garden."

"You mean weeding? Yuck!"

"Billy, how badly do you want that bike?"

2

By the time lunch was over, Billy had made up his mind. He'd just have to earn the money for a new bike.

Billy found Howard sweeping out the Rosas' garage. "Howard, do you know if there are any paper routes like yours I could get?"

"Gee," said Howard. "I think they're all taken."

Billy shoved his hands in his pockets. "I have to find some kind of job."

Howard stopped sweeping and leaned on the broom. "Did your parents say no to buying you a bike?"

"They're paying for a new roof, so they can't right now."

"Hey! You know what? There's a sign for

a job in Uncle Spaghetti's window."

"The pizza man?"

"Yeah. No—wait a minute. I heard he's a pain to work for. But last week the Petersons asked if I'd take care of their pets while they're away."

"Are you going to?"

"I can't. I'm allergic to cats."

"Wow! Maybe I could."

"Mrs. Peterson'll probably give you a thousand things to do. She's nuts about her pets."

"But it's a job," said Billy.

"So, go talk to her."

"Thanks. See ya later." Billy hurried down Lee Avenue.

"Hello there, young man," a high and fluttery voice called out.

Billy stopped in front of a big white house. Mrs. Lowell was the oldest person on the street. Every summer she sat on her porch and watched the neighborhood kids. "Hi, Mrs. Lowell," Billy said.

Her big brown dog hobbled down the front steps. He wagged his tail and sniffed at Billy's sneakers.

"How're you doing, Bowser?" Billy scratched the old dog's head. Bowser whined and licked Billy's hand.

"Mrs. Lowell, if you ever need anyone to take care of Bowser when you go on vacation, I'll do it."

"Thank you, dear, but I always take him. He sits right next to me in the front seat of the car. In fact, tomorrow we're driving to my daughter's summer home. I just hope Howard remembers not to deliver the newspapers. Last time he forgot, and they blew all over the yard."

"I'll remind him," said Billy. Then he had another thought. "Maybe I could walk Bowser for you on rainy days."

"Thank you, Billy, but I really like getting out myself."

Too bad, Billy thought. No job here. "Well, 'bye, Mrs. Lowell. Have a nice vacation."

Billy crossed the street in front of the Petersons' brick house. He didn't know Mrs. P. that well, but she always waved when she was out trying to walk her big black cat. Billy rang the bell.

Mrs. Peterson was a large woman with frizzy reddish hair. "Hi," said Billy. "Howard told me you needed a pet sitter."

She nodded. "Yes, but it must be someone who adores animals."

"I do! And I'm really *good* with them."

"Well, I don't know," she said, sounding doubtful.

"I used to help out at the vet's," Billy added quickly.

"Why don't I show you what has to be done? Then we'll decide."

"Sure," said Billy. He followed Mrs. Peterson into the kitchen.

"The cat'll need his water and litter changed daily. The food's in here." Mrs. Peterson opened a wooden door under the sink.

The door had long, deep scratches, the kind a big cat makes. Billy glanced around. There was stuffing hanging out of one kitchen chair. He'd seen a cat do that kind of thing. "Is your cat friendly?"

"Oh, Choo-Choo's a dear, once he gets to know you. I keep him indoors except when I

walk him. I'm afraid he'll get hurt if he goes
out alone."

From the look of things, Billy thought,
Choo-Choo wouldn't be the one in danger.

"Here, Choo-Choo. Oh, Choo!" Mrs. Peterson called. "Isn't that typical? Cats never
come." She headed into the dining room.
"Here's Sidney. He's our other darling."

"Sidney?"

The parakeet sat chirping in his cage. "Hi, sweet Sid." Mrs. Peterson made chirping sounds. The bird stared at her blankly and moved to the far end of his perch.

"He'll need water and food each day," Mrs. Peterson continued. "And whatever you do, don't let him out. Sid wouldn't have a chance around Choo."

Mrs. Peterson scratched her head. "Let's see, is there anything else I should tell you? I guess we can skip having you brush Choo's teeth. We'll only be gone a week."

Billy tried not to laugh. "The vet only did *her* cats' teeth once a year," he said.

"Humph!" said Mrs. Peterson. "We're more careful than that. Well, Billy, do you think you can handle it?"

The bird would be a cinch. Choo-Choo might be nasty. But, Billy figured, if he wanted a bike, it might mean doing hard stuff. Besides, what other job was there? "I'll do it," he said.

"My animals must be treated with love, Billy."

"I'll take real good care of them."

"All right, then. Is there anything else I can tell you?"

"When do I start?"

Mrs. Peterson laughed. "Of course. First thing Saturday morning. We'll be back the following Friday." She opened the door.

He had to find out about the money.

"Now be careful with the key."

"Umm...Mrs. Peterson, how much could you pay—"

"Oh, yes! How's thirty-five dollars when we get back?"

"Wow, that's great!"

"We always pay well. We want the best. They're our darlings."

She was a little weird, Billy thought, but thirty-five dollars! *That* was too good to be true.

3

Ten mountain bikes in metallic reds, greens, and purples were on display in Ronson's window. The two black ones with purple trim and alloy rims were the coolest–looking, Billy thought.

He read the sign in the window. SALE RUNS SATURDAY TO SATURDAY. LOWEST PRICES EVER! MOUNTAIN BIKES—$139!

Oh, no! Billy thought. The sale started in just two days. The thirty-five dollars from the Petersons, plus the seventeen in his piggy bank, made fifty-two dollars. Not even half the price of a bike. He needed more money and he needed it fast.

Billy looked around at the other Main Street stores. There was a bakery, a shoe store,

a deli. Hey—the ice cream shop! He knew the guy who ran it.

As Billy came through the open door, the heavyset man behind the counter looked up. "What flavor today, Billy?"

"No thanks, Mr. Hutson. I was wondering if you might need someone to sweep and take out garbage and stuff."

"No, sorry. My son does that at night after we close."

Billy nodded. Outside, he watched people on the street. What else could he do? There had to be something.

On the glass door of Uncle Spaghetti's Pizza Parlor was a little handwritten sign. Billy walked over. HELP WANTED. INQUIRE WITHIN.

Howard said Uncle Spaghetti was a pain. But if it meant getting a mountain bike, Billy figured he'd try anything.

He peered in the window. It was pretty quiet inside, with only one woman and her little girl sitting at a table. Billy opened the door.

A tall man in a white hat shouted, "Yeah, what'll it be?"

"I saw the sign," Billy said timidly. "You still need help?"

"I'll get Uncle Spaghetti. Wait here." The white hat disappeared.

Billy heard talking in the back. Then a small, tubby old man came around the counter. He was frowning. "You! I was thinking someone with a car."

"Oh," said Billy.

"I need fliers put in all the mailboxes in the business area and the neighborhoods by Sunday. That's when the discount for senior citizens starts."

"I can do that."

"Hmm," said Uncle Spaghetti, looking Billy over. "I'll check to make sure you deliver all of them."

"I'm sure I can do it," said Billy. "What could you pay me?"

"Five cents a flier."

"A nickel!" exclaimed Billy. At this rate, it would take the rest of his life to get a bike.

The man's face turned red. "You calling Uncle Spaghetti *cheap*?"

"No," said Billy, a little scared.

"Sonny boy, if you deliver all five hundred fliers, you'll make twenty-five dollars."

Gee! Twenty-five plus thirty-five was… uh…sixty, and with the money in his piggy bank the total came to seventy-seven dollars. *More than half!* "I'll do it," said Billy.

"Tomorrow's Friday. Be here at ten sharp. Not a minute later. You'll have two days to deliver the fliers."

Billy started out for home. Seventy-seven dollars was great, but still not enough. Where could he earn the rest?

Think, brain, think! If he got the fliers done

tomorrow, and if he took care of the pets in the mornings, he could work afternoons, too. His grandmother would pay him to weed her flower beds. Yuck, weeding! But to get his bike, it would be worth it.

"Yo, Bill!" Howard came over the rise, slowed, then braked right in front of Billy. "Do I ever have something for you!"

"What I need, Howard, is money."

"My man!" Howard laughed. "I just found out we're going up to my uncle's cabin. Want to do my paper route for a week?"

"Are you kidding?"

"You'd have to start tomorrow, but you could make an easy fifty plus tips."

"Yes!" said Billy, socking the air with his fist.

"I figured you'd say that."

Seventy-seven plus fifty was...one hundred and twenty-seven. He'd only have to earn twelve dollars to have enough. Howard talked about earning that much in tips all the time.

"Now I really *can* buy that bike! I'm taking care of the Petersons' pets and I got a job with Uncle Spaghetti."

Howard made a face. "You're going to work for *him*?"

"Delivering fliers."

"Petersons, newspapers, *and* fliers! Three jobs?" Howard was shocked.

"Yeah. I'm hoping it'll be okay. I figure the fliers will take one day. Two days, max. And I only have to go to the Petersons' in the morning."

"Do my papers first, okay? People get angry if they're late."

"Sure thing." Billy grinned at his friend. "This is my lucky day! I can't believe it's so easy to earn money."

"We'll be charging over those reservoir trails any day now, Bill."

"Oh, man!" said Billy. "Think about the rocks and the dropoffs."

"I know," Howard said. "It'll be great."

Billy found his mother seated at the picnic table in the backyard. Baby Sarah sat on the grass, throwing clumps of dirt in the air.

"Billy! Billy!" Sarah barreled across the yard.

"Hi, Sarah." Billy patted her head. There were twigs and leaves in her hair.

"Where've you been all afternoon?" his mother asked.

"I got some jobs so I can buy a bike like Howard's."

"Oh really?" said Mrs. Getten. "What kind of jobs?"

"Taking care of the Petersons' pets and dropping fliers in mailboxes for Uncle Spaghetti. Oh, and delivering for Howard."

His mother raised her eyebrows. "That sounds like a lot, Bill, and I'm afraid I'm going to ask you to change your plans a little."

"Why?" said Billy. "What for?"

"To mind Sarah in the mornings. The roofer called back and said he'd give us a discount if we ripped the rotted shingles off ourselves. We're going to work mornings while it's cool, so we'll need your help."

"Oh, Mom," Billy groaned.

Mrs. Getten looked at Sarah, who was chasing bugs. She sighed. "I know, but it'll only be for a few days. Your father and I have to do the work now, while we're both on vacation."

"Can you pay me, at least?"

"Sweetie, you know we don't do that. And you get an allowance."

"When do I have to start?"

"The day after tomorrow."

Just then Sarah plopped down in the grass. She put something in her mouth and began chewing.

"Mom! Did you see that?"

Mrs. Getten went over and sat beside Sarah. "Let me see, honey. What do you have in there?"

Sarah stuck out her tongue.

"Oh, gross," said Billy. Even his mother looked sick when she lifted out the half-chewed grasshopper.

4

Very early Friday morning, the sun peeked through the clouds. Birds rustled the leaves in the tree outside Billy's window. It was a perfect day, he thought, to be out in the woods on a mountain bike.

"Come on, Stewie," Billy whispered to his dog. Everyone in the family was still asleep. "We've got work to do." They slipped out of Billy's house.

Okay, Billy thought, papers first, then, after breakfast, Uncle Spaghetti. Pet-feeding doesn't start till tomorrow. Not bad.

A pile of papers in a clear plastic bag lay on the walk. Rats! He'd forgotten Howard's canvas carrier. Too late to go back now.

Billy lifted the bundle and the plastic ripped. Newspapers slid all over the ground. The wind blew one into the bushes and another into the gutter.

"Oh, great! Come, Stewie." Billy pointed to the pile. "Sit." The dog climbed on.

The sports section of one newspaper got a little ripped when Billy pulled it out of the bushes. The coupons in the other were damp from the wet gutter.

After he had folded all the papers, just the way Howard did, Billy loaded his arms. Halfway down the block, he dropped a bunch. "Geez."

He bent over and dropped more. "Here, Stewie, you carry some."

At the Rockwells' house, Billy wiped off Stewie's saliva and shoved a paper into the mail drop. Howard's little brown book said the Sheppards next door had gone away. He skipped them.

Mrs. Lowell's car was parked on the street. She hadn't left for vacation yet. Billy flung a paper onto her porch. Inside, Bowser barked.

Stewie's tail wagged. He barked back.

"Shush. You'll wake Mrs. Lowell. Come on, we have more to do."

An hour later, Billy had ink smudges on his hands and shirt. His arms ached. Two papers were left. Howard hadn't said anything about leftovers. Billy tucked them under his arm and started home.

"Just one minute, young man!" a deep voice called.

Billy looked around. He didn't see anyone. He kept walking.

"I'm talking to you, Billy Getten!" A man in a plaid bathrobe stood in the doorway. "Did you deliver this morning?"

"Yes, Mr. Sheppard."

"Well, you forgot me!"

Billy checked Howard's book. "Gee, it says you're still away."

"I told Howard we'd be back today."

"He must have forgotten to put it down."

"Make sure you deliver our paper tomorrow. I read the news first thing over coffee."

Billy nodded and handed him one of the

leftover papers. Once Mr. Sheppard's door had slammed, Billy whispered to Stewie, "What a grouch."

A little while later, Billy walked into the kitchen. His mother put down her cup of coffee. "Hi! How'd it go?"

"Good." Billy grabbed his favorite cereal

and a bowl. He sat down at the round table with his parents and sister.

"Billy," his father said, "we'd like you to watch Sarah today."

"Oh, no!"

"It's going to rain tomorrow," his father continued. "Maybe even later today. So we want to get started on the roof this morning."

"But I've got to deliver Uncle Spaghetti's fliers today."

"Take Sarah with you," Mrs. Getten said.

Billy groaned. "I have all this walking to do. She can't keep up."

Mrs. Getten laughed. "Put her in the red wagon. She'll be fine."

"That squeaky thing?"

Mr. Getten stood up and pushed his chair in. "You can haul the fliers around in the wagon, too."

There wasn't enough money in the world to make it worth watching Sarah, thought Billy. And now he had to do it *for nothing*. There was drool on her chin and banana in her hair. What if the kids from school saw him?

Billy's mother patted his hand. "I'll clean her up."

Billy rolled his eyes. "Swell."

Not long after, he pulled Sarah and the squeaky wagon down the driveway. She was singing quietly. He knew that wouldn't last.

"Wait, Billy," his mother called from the kitchen window.

"Now what?"

"Mrs. O'Brien's on the phone. She says she didn't get her paper."

The other leftover paper! "Tell her I'll bring it later."

"Now, Billy!" his father called from the roof.

"Okay, okay." What difference did another ten minutes make? He was already late for Uncle Spaghetti's anyway.

5

On Main Street, Sarah sang and waved to the cars. "Hi! Hi! Hi!" she shouted.

"Sarah, cut it out." Billy hated the way she'd talk to everyone in the world.

"Hey, I'm three years old!" screamed Sarah.

A truck driver smiled. He waved three fingers out the window. Sarah waved back.

Once the light changed, Billy crossed. Maybe while he was dropping off fliers, he could stop and talk with Mr. Ronson, the bike shop owner.

A man coming out of the pizza parlor held the door open. "Thanks," Billy said, and pulled the noisy wagon over the threshold.

Uncle Spaghetti was sitting at one of the

empty tables. He looked up from his newspaper and frowned. "You're late. And who's this?"

"My sister."

"You're dragging a baby around?"

"Pizza! Pizza!" Sarah said.

"It's her favorite word."

Sarah blew him a kiss. "Hi, Grandpa!" she cooed.

The old man smiled. He picked up a stack of fliers and handed them to Billy. "Don't forget the senior citizens' center. They get the special discount starting Sunday."

"Okay." Billy shoved the fliers under his arm. Walking backward, he pulled the wagon to the door, held the door open with one hand, and yanked the wagon outside. The fliers fell to the ground.

"My fliers!" Uncle Spaghetti came running to the door.

A gust of wind picked up two fliers and carried them down the street. "There's ten cents you're not getting from me, young man."

Billy stamped his foot on the others to keep them from getting away.

"And I'm not paying for dirty ones, either."

"I'll be careful, I promise." Billy shoved the fliers into a ragged pile. Uncle Spaghetti grumbled and went back inside.

A gang of older boys was sitting on a nearby stoop. "Man," one said, laughing. "Is he paying you in old pizza crusts?" Another shouted, "His pizza's the worst!" He stuck a finger in his mouth and pretended to throw up.

"My bike, my bike," Billy mumbled to himself.

Some of the fliers had landed under a parked car. Billy pulled the wagon closer to the curb.

"Sarah, just hold these fliers on your lap."

"Pizza! Pizza!" she shouted.

"And be quiet!"

As Billy knelt down, Sarah tossed the fliers into the air. They swirled around in the wind and blew along the sidewalk.

There was a roar of laughter from the stoop. "Way to go, kid!"

Billy wanted to die. He ran around collecting the fliers again. If Uncle Spaghetti was

looking out the window, Billy knew, he'd be
dead for real.

Just then there was a clap of thunder.
"Bill-eee!" Sarah screeched.

It figured! It was going to rain. He didn't
have a jacket on, or anything with him to
protect the fliers. He tucked them under his
T-shirt and held an arm against his chest to
keep them in place. Now there was no way he
could get the fliers passed out today.

He began running, pulling the wagon with

one hand and holding the fliers with the other.
The fliers kept slipping down, and the wagon
was squeaking like crazy.

"Faster! Faster!" Sarah shouted.

"My bike, my bike," Billy reminded himself
as the rain began beating down.

6

The rain continued all that day and night. It was still coming down on Saturday morning when Billy started delivering the newspapers. He got soaked making sure the papers stayed dry, but he didn't mind. If it kept on raining, his parents couldn't work on the roof, and he wouldn't be stuck with Sarah.

However, during breakfast the rain stopped. Billy knew there was no point in mentioning that it might start raining again. His mother had Sarah waiting in the wagon. Mrs. Getten had even put the fliers in a plastic shopping bag.

Billy pulled the wagon down the driveway. Stewie started barking.

"Stay, Stewie," Billy said. "I can't take you with me."

Stewie whined.

"I know, buddy. I wish you could come, too."

Stewie's tail hung low. Billy headed down the driveway.

"'Bye, Billy. 'Bye, Sarah!" Mrs. Getten called from the roof.

"See you later!" his father yelled, climbing out a window. "And thanks."

"Pizza!" Sarah said. "I'm hungry."

First, Billy thought, he'd take care of the pets, then deliver the fliers. If he didn't finish them by this afternoon, Uncle Spaghetti would never pay him the twenty-five dollars.

"Bill-eee," Sarah wailed. "Pizza!"

"Listen, you." Billy leaned over his sister. "Mom said you have to do what I say."

"Pizza!" Sarah threw the plastic shopping bag on the ground. A few fliers slid out.

"Don't do that!" Billy picked up everything. If only he'd brought a banana or something for her.

Sarah pounded her heels on the floor of the wagon. "I want pizza!"

"Sarah," Billy said, as calmly as he could, "do you want to do something else that's good?"

"What?"

"I can't tell you yet, but if you want to, you have to behave."

Sarah eyed him suspiciously, but she quieted down.

Bowser barked as they passed Mrs. Lowell's house. Her car was in the driveway. She still hadn't left for vacation. Good thing he'd dropped off a paper earlier, he thought.

Next to Mrs. Lowell's house, a stout woman leaned over the fence. "Young man! I'd like a word with you."

"Yes, Mrs. Warner." Billy halted the wagon on the sidewalk.

"This won't do." Between two fingers, Mrs. Warner held out a dripping wet newspaper. "There's no way I can read this. I keep telling you kids to put the newspaper in plastic when it rains."

"But I did," Billy said.

Mrs. Warner squinted at him. "Does this look wrapped to you?"

This morning he'd slipped every paper into a clear wrapper. Billy stared at the soggy mess. "Mrs. Warner, I delivered the *Capital.* That's the *Record.*"

The woman glared at him. Then she turned and walked away.

Boy, thought Billy. Why did Howard call this job easy?

At the Petersons' house, Billy unlocked the back door and led Sarah into the kitchen. "Now, listen, I want you to sit on this chair. *And don't move!*"

"Salt, pepper, sugar." Sarah pointed to the table.

"Don't touch anything, either."

Choo-Choo, the cat, was nowhere around. Good, Billy thought.

He found the litter box in the bathroom next to the kitchen. Holding his nose, Billy cleaned the box out with a scoop. He flushed everything down the toilet. "Yuck!"

"Good Sarah," Billy said as he came back

into the kitchen. She was still in her chair.

Billy rinsed the cat's water bowl with warm water, then refilled it with cold water. The dry cat food was under the sink. He opened the scratched wooden door and pulled out the bag.

Suddenly there was a crash. "Bill-eee!"

"Sarah!" The kitchen chair was empty. "Sarah, where are you?"

In the dining room, Sarah stood on a chair. The bird-cage stand was on the floor. The cage was open—and there was no bird in it.

"Sar-ah! How did Sid get out?" Oh, man, he didn't need this.

Sarah giggled. "Birdie."

Sid flew across the room. He landed on Sarah's head.

"Don't move," Billy said with gritted teeth. If he could just get Sidney on his finger, everything would be okay. He reached out a hand. "Come on, little guy," he said.

The bird flew around the room. He landed on the rug.

"I'm hungry," Sarah said.

"We'll get pizza," Billy told her, feeling

desperate. "Just stay still."

"No!" Sarah climbed down and marched into the kitchen.

Sid pecked at the rug. Billy got down on his hands and knees. "Come, sweet Sid." He made chirping sounds, the way Mrs. Peterson had.

Suddenly the bird squawked.

Choo-Choo, looking like a small panther, stood in the doorway.

"You!" Billy clapped his hands. "Get out of here!"

Choo-Choo crouched on all fours. His back end began wiggling.

"No!" Billy shouted.

The cat sprang.

Sid flew straight up and into a window. He tumbled to the floor.

Choo-Choo licked his chops.

"Oh no you don't!" Billy shouted.

Choo-Choo growled.

Very, very slowly Billy leaned toward Sid. Even more slowly, he reached out for him.

The cat bared his fangs and hissed.

Billy pulled back.

Sid's wings fluttered.

Choo-Choo crouched again, his tail slithering like a snake.

Sid soared into the air and landed on top of the drapes.

Billy took a deep breath. The bird was safe.

But Sid didn't stay put. He let out a squawk and dove at the cat. Choo-Choo swiped at him but missed.

Sid zoomed toward the ceiling and did another dive-bomb. This time he nicked the cat's ear.

"Aoow!" Choo-Choo howled and fled down the hall.

Billy stood up and lifted the overturned cage.

Sid flew gracefully around the room and then back toward his cage. He hopped inside, settled on his perch, and began chirping.

Billy took a deep, deep breath. He closed the cage door, but he couldn't help smiling. Sid had probably waited years to let that cat have it.

"Oh, Billy!" Sarah called.

"Sarah!" *Now* where was she? Choo-Choo had headed into the kitchen. Billy hurried down the hall.

Sarah sat in the middle of the kitchen floor. She had ripped open the bag of dry cat food. Little brown pellets lay scattered all over.

Sarah popped a handful in her mouth. "Here, kitty, have some."

Billy couldn't move. The cat sniffed Sarah's hand. Then he glared at Billy and hissed. Finally Choo-Choo took the food and crunched it.

"Good kitty," Sarah said, petting the cat's head. Choo-Choo curled up next to her and began to purr.

"Only you could get away with that, Sarah," Billy said.

Sarah looked up and smiled. "I'm having fun."

"Swell!" Billy said. He looked at the kitchen floor, then over his shoulder at the disaster in the dining room. Bird seed and bird poop lay all over. Thirty-five dollars for this? He'd better find some paper towels and a broom.

7

An hour later, Billy trudged up Lee Avenue
with Sarah in tow. He decided to deliver a few
fliers on his walk home and then finish them
after lunch. Tomorrow he'd do the papers and
the Petersons' pets *before* taking Sarah out. No
way was he taking her back to the Petersons'
again! Only the thought of the mountain bike
kept him going.

As he put a flier in Mrs. Lowell's mailbox,
he heard Bowser barking like crazy. Wondering what was going on, Billy stopped to listen.
He parked the wagon at the foot of the porch
steps. "Don't get out," he told his sister. She
took some cat food out of her pocket and
popped it in her mouth.

Billy climbed the creaky steps and peered

through a front window. The lace curtains made it hard to see.

He rang the bell. Inside, Bowser jumped against the door.

The newspaper was still on the mat. Why hadn't Mrs. Lowell picked it up? It was almost noon.

Billy pulled the wagon around the side of the house. "Hello!" he called, knocking at the back door. Bowser barked again.

Maybe Mrs. Lowell had decided not to go on vacation today. Or maybe she had left Bowser home. But she'd said that she always took him. What if she was in trouble or sick?

Bowser pawed the glass and howled.

Something was wrong, Billy thought. He tried the door. It was locked. He tried one of the windows. It was locked, too.

Bowser let out another howl.

"I'll get help, boy. I'll get help." Billy grabbed the handle of the wagon and started running. "Hang on, Sarah!" They charged around to the front of the house.

"Mrs. Warner!" Billy called over the fence. "I think there's something wrong at Mrs. Lowell's. Bowser's barking too much."

Mrs. Warner looked up from her roses. "That dog is always barking," she said. "It's so annoying. I wouldn't worry if I were you."

Billy looked back at the house. Maybe Mrs. Warner was right. Maybe he was being dumb. Then Bowser let out another yelp. "Mrs. Warner, could I use your phone? I have to call my mother."

"All right. It's just inside the back door."

"Could you watch Sarah for a second?"

Mrs. Warner frowned. "For a moment," she said.

The phone rang a long time at Billy's house. Both of his parents must be up on the roof. Finally, Mrs. Getten panted, "Hello?"

"Mom, listen. I think something's wrong with Mrs. Lowell. She told me she was going away yesterday, but her car's still here. And she hasn't picked up her newspaper. And Bowser's barking his head off inside, and all the doors are locked."

"Billy, where are you? Where's Sarah?"

"At Mrs. Warner's. Sarah's with her."

"Billy, I'll call the police. Wait outside.

We'll be right there." Billy heard his mother shout for his dad as she hung up the phone. She didn't even say good-bye.

An ambulance and a police car were parked outside Mrs. Lowell's house. A crowd of neighbors waited with Billy and his parents. When Mrs. Lowell's front door opened, a policeman stepped out. "Does anyone know the family?"

"Is Mrs. Lowell all right?" Billy asked.

"Yes. She fell in her kitchen. She has a broken leg."

"Oh, I feel terrible," said Mrs. Warner. "I'll phone her daughter."

"A window needs to be boarded up," the policeman said. "We broke it to get in."

"We can take care of that," said Mr. Sheppard. Billy's father nodded.

"Mom," said Billy, "should we keep Bowser with us?"

"Yes, of course."

The policeman looked at Billy. "Are you the boy?"

Billy nodded, feeling a little scared.

"You did a good thing, son. You deserve a

reward of some kind."

"Gee," said Billy. "Thanks."

The front door opened again. The ambulance attendants wheeled the stretcher across the porch. Mrs. Lowell was all bundled up in green blankets. Her eyes were wide open and sparkling.

"Mrs. Lowell!" Billy said.

She smiled. "Thank you," she answered in her fluttery voice.

The ambulance drivers carried her down the stairs.

8

For the rest of the week, Billy delivered Howard's newspapers and took care of the Petersons' pets. Somehow, he managed to mind Sarah while keeping Bowser and Stewie from running off into the woods together.

On Saturday morning, he got back from delivering newspapers and slumped against the kitchen door. "Billy!" his mother said, holding open the newspaper. "You're famous."

"Yeah, everyone stopped me to talk about the article."

"I love the picture of you shaking hands with the police captain. I hope we can get copies."

"I wish they'd given me money instead of a badge."

"Billy, don't be greedy," his mother said. "You've had three calls this morning to do some jobs for that senior citizens' group."

Billy sighed. The last thing he wanted was another job.

"Listen, I have good news. Your father and I should be finished with the roof today, so you'll only have to watch Sarah for an hour."

"Swell," said Billy.

"Oh, and Mrs. Lowell's daughter called. She said Mrs. Lowell's home from the hospital and doing fine. And Uncle Spaghetti said—"

"He called?"

"He wants you to stop in."

"Mom, he's going to kill me!" With all the excitement at Mrs. Lowell's, Billy had never noticed that the fliers were missing from his wagon. The next morning when he was delivering newspapers, he'd found the shopping bag under a bush. The rain had seeped in and ruined most of the fliers.

"Go talk to him. Maybe you're wrong."

"Yeah, maybe," Billy said, but he knew he wasn't wrong at all.

After breakfast, Billy headed down the driveway, pulling the wagon. "Whee!" Sarah shouted.

"Yo, Bill, wait up." Howard's bike slid to a stop.

"Hi! When'd you get back?"

"Last night. This is for you." Howard held out an envelope.

"What is it?"

"Your money. I went around and collected. You did great on tips!"

Billy shrugged. "Thanks." He shoved the money into his jeans pocket without even looking at it.

"Hey, what's wrong? That's sixty-two dollars!"

Billy sighed. "I still don't have enough for the bike."

"What do you mean? I thought you said you could do it."

"Yeah, well, Uncle Spaghetti's fliers got ruined. So I never delivered them."

"What'd he say?"

"I never told him."

"Whoa!"

"Yeah. I'll probably have to pay for the fliers."

Howard shook his head. "How much money do you have?"

"Everything together comes to"—Billy added quickly—"umm...a hundred and fourteen dollars."

"How much is the bike?"

"A hundred and thirty-nine."

"So all you need is that twenty-five dollars. I've got four in my train bank you could have."

Billy shook his head. "Thanks, but there's no way I can do it. All because of those fliers."

"Oh, come on! You're so close. Don't give up. Let's go talk to him." Howard walked his bike. Billy pulled the wagon.

"Hiya! Hiya!" Sarah yelled.

They stopped in front of Ronson's. The sign said, "Last Day." A single mountain bike was left. It was Billy's favorite, the black one with purple trim.

"Oh, man," Billy moaned.

"Hi," said Mr. Ronson. "Interested in that bike?"

"Yeah," said Billy. "But I don't have

enough money yet. You couldn't save it for me for a couple of days?"

Mr. Ronson shook his head. "I'd like to help you, but I can't really. If someone comes in, I've got to sell it. I have a new shipment coming in today. I have to have room."

"Are you sure?" asked Howard. "It's only one bike."

"Yes. Sorry."

Billy nodded. All that work. He pulled the wagon up Main Street. Howard followed.

"Pizza!" Sarah shouted as they came to Uncle Spaghetti's.

The door to the pizza parlor was open. "Billy!" yelled Uncle Spaghetti. "Where have you been?"

Here it comes, thought Billy. The unluckiest day of my life. "Um, Uncle Spaghetti, I have something to tell you. I—"

"Billy," the old man interrupted, "the phone hasn't stopped ringing since we opened. Look at this place! It's mobbed."

Billy looked around. It was true. Every table was full. Lots of senior citizens were having lunch.

"You must have mentioned me five times in that newspaper article. I got terrific publicity from it. And the lady you helped, she's been telling all her friends about the specials for senior citizens."

"Really?" said Billy. He looked at Howard.

Howard elbowed Billy.

"So, now—what did you want to tell me?" Uncle Spaghetti said.

Billy hesitated a moment, but he knew he had to tell even if it cost him the bike. "Well, see, I never really finished delivering all of the fliers. And some of them..." Billy's voice trailed off when he saw the old man's frown.

"Yeah," Howard added quickly, "but if he *had* finished them, he never would have been the one to save Mrs. Lowell, and the article never would have been written about him, and you wouldn't have been in the paper five times, and..." Howard's voice faded, too.

Uncle Spaghetti's face was very red. He opened his mouth, but nothing came out.

"Oh, Grandpa," Sarah piped up, "I love pizza."

Uncle Spaghetti looked at Sarah. Very slowly, as if against his will, a smile spread across his face. He cleared his throat.

Sarah held her arms wide open. "This much."

"You want a slice?"

Sarah nodded.

Without a word, Uncle Spaghetti went and got a slice of pizza. Billy looked at Howard. Howard shrugged. They watched him give Sarah a huge piece. And then he reached into his pocket.

"Well, Billy," said the old man, "even though you didn't finish, here's the twenty-five dollars."

"Really?" Billy said.

"Make sure I've counted it right."

"Oh, you counted it right! Thanks," said Billy.

Billy and Howard hurried the wagon out the door. On the sidewalk, Howard gave Billy a high five. "You did it, buddy. Let's go."

"Pizza! Pizza!" Sarah shouted as they headed for the bike shop. She had cheese on her chin and sauce on her shirt. Nobody cared.

Billy shifted gears on his shiny black Predator with the purple trim. Howard adjusted his new micro-pump helmet.

They crossed the road and headed into the woods toward the reservoir. A narrow, rocky path brought them down a steep embankment and onto the aqueduct trail.

"Wooo-eee!" cried Billy, crashing through the low brush.

They sailed along the grassy path.

Billy called out, "If we leave the trail here, the stream in the woods is right below us."

"Want to ride it down to the bottom?" asked Howard. "We'd come out at the reservoir."

"You're on." Billy laughed.

They dove down through the trees, crashing into thickets and weaving around boulders. Billy narrowly missed a car tire.

All the rain had swollen the stream, so Billy couldn't see the rocks he knew were there, under the water. He hesitated for just a second.

Then he hunkered down and charged into the stream. Muddy water splashed his face, and what he swallowed tasted bitter.

He hit a rock and his teeth rattled, but nothing could stop him or his mountain bike.

Howard whooshed alongside him. Billy shivered from the cold spray. The place where the

stream went underground was coming up fast.

Billy let out a shout. He flew up the muddy bank, out of the woods and into the sunlight.

He was covered with mud. Even his teeth were muddy. His parents would kill him.

"Is this the best or what?" Howard called.

"Let's do it again!" yelled Billy.

About the Author

BETSY SACHS based some of *Mountain Bike Madness* on her own childhood. "I always had lots of jobs while I was growing up, just like Billy Getten," she says. "I also owned a cat named Choo-Choo, but he was even meaner than the one in the book. He'd bite you and purr at the same time!" Betsy Sachs is the author of many books for children, including *The Boy Who Ate Dog Biscuits,* another Stepping Stone Book starring Billy Getten.

MOUNTAIN
BIKES
$139.!

About the Illustrator

PENNY DANN likes to visit schools and draw for students. "I always tell kids they're never too young to become artists. My mum says I started drawing when I was only two—and I've been doing it ever since!" Penny Dann is the illustrator of many books for adults and children, including *Brutus the Wonder Poodle,* a Stepping Stone Book. She lives in London, England, with her three cats.